FERGUS - FABULOUS FERRET

Alison Prince

Illustrated by
Caroline Jayne Church

Hodder
Children's
Books

a division of Hodder Headline plc

A Catalogue record for this book is available from the British Library

ISBN 0340 69369 X

Printed and bound in Great Britain by
Mackays of Chatham PLC, Chatham, Kent

Hodder Children's Books
A Division of Hodder Headline plc
338 Euston Road
London NW1 3BH

Chapter One

Martin lived in a flat, right at
the top of a
tall building.
His mum
and dad
were always
staring out
of the
window
through
binoculars
because
they liked
watching
birds.

Martin couldn't see why they bothered. There were plenty of birds down in the car park, eating crisps and bits of bread – easy to see without binoculars – but his parents said birds like that were *common*.

Martin couldn't see the difference between common birds and uncommon ones. They all whizzed past the window very fast and dropped white sploshes on the balcony, and they never looked like

their pictures in his parents'
bird books. Altogether they
were pretty boring. His parents
had bought
Martin a pair
of budgies, but
they weren't
much better.
They were
supposed to talk,
but they never did, just sat side
by side on their
perch and
stared at the
television.
Martin called
them Beeb
and Ighty.

Sometimes they ate a bit of
bird seed or kissed each other,
but they weren't much
interested in Martin.
He wanted a
proper pet,
with fur and a
feeding bowl
and four legs.
Something that
would sleep on
his bed. A dog,
perhaps, or
a cat.

Martin mentioned this to his
dad, who frowned. "What if a
passing albatross should see a
dog or a cat looking out of the

window?" he said. "It might die of fright."

"Um," said Martin. He thought an alba-whatnot could be just as frightened by seeing a man looking at it through binoculars, but decided not to say so.

His mum joined in. "And anyway, you've got the budgies," she said. "They're nice, aren't they? Even if they don't talk yet."

Martin nodded. Actually, he liked Mrs Toffee better than the budgies. Mrs Toffee was a large spider who lived on the curtain rail in his bedroom.

If he blew
gently at the
corner of her
web, she'd
come rush-
ing out,
looking all
excited.
Sometimes he'd give her a fly
he'd managed to catch, and
she'd wrap it up in a sticky
parcel and hide it away in her
store. That's why he called
her Mrs Toffee, because of the
sticky stuff. She was more fun
than the budgies, but he'd
still have liked a dog or a cat.
Or a ferret.

Martin's Auntie Fan had a ferret. His name was Fergus. Auntie Fan was a comfortable person, dumpy and round like a tea cosy. She wore an old hat with a feather in it and this fur draped round her neck – only it wasn't a fur, it was Fergus.

He had fur, of course, all over, a nice brown colour, a black nose and bright black eyes, round ears and neat little claws on his hands and feet. He was very long and thin, especially if you included his tail, and his white teeth were extremely sharp. He never bit people, though. Well – not on purpose, anyway.

Chapter Two

One Friday afternoon, Martin
came home from school to find
his parents ramming things
into rucksacks. They had
maps open on the table,

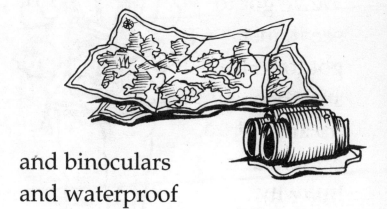

and binoculars
and waterproof

gloves and
woolly hats.

"A flat-footed mudwit!" his dad said. "Spotted in Clodshire Marshes this morning – must have been blown off course from Gdansk. We've got to see it, just got to." He snatched up another camera and hung it round his neck with the others.

"So you'll be away for the weekend," said Martin, who was used to this.

His mum looked up from pulling her boots on. "Yes. You don't mind, love, do you? Pop down and tell Mrs Handy you'll be there until tomorrow night, there's a good boy. Explain that it's an emergency. You can take what's in the fridge."

"Mrs Handy's not there any more," said Martin. "She moved away to the seaside."

13

"Really?" His dad seemed startled. "Oh, yes, she did mention it. I remember telling her to look out for a red-eyed winkler-picker. You get them at the coast sometimes."

"She's not into birds," said Martin. "She just said she was fed up with emergencies. Can I go and stay with Auntie Fan?"

His parents looked at each other. "He'll come back smelling of ferret," said his mum. "He always does."

His dad shrugged. "Can't be helped. I mean this *is* an emergency. Get your stuff together, Martin.

We'll drop you off on the way.
But hurry up, we don't want
to miss this mudwit."

Martin made a
quick phone call
to Auntie Fan,
who laughed
about the mudwit
and said he was
very welcome. Martin and his
parents and their binoculars
got into the lift – which was
working for once –
and went down
to the car park,
leaving the
television on for
the budgies.

Auntie Fan's road was what she called Nice. It had been widened and a lot of new houses had been built, with big lawns and no privet hedges, and front doors with white pillars on either side and important steps. Auntie Fan's house wasn't like that. It was an old cottage that had been

there ever since the road was just a narrow lane. Her garden was full of bushes and daisies and weeds because it was getting a bit much for her to manage. Martin's parents said it was ecological and great for birds so the weedier the better, but the neighbours with the big lawns didn't like it a bit.

Auntie Fan came to the door with Fergus round her neck. "Good luck with the mudwit," she said to Martin's parents. "But won't it be dark when you get there?"

"Oh yes," said Martin's dad. "That's the point, though. We need to get ourselves a place, you see –

behind a tree or in a ditch, preferably. There'll be a lot of people trying to see the bird. We'll get a few hours' sleep, then be up before dawn, ready for it.'

"I'm sure you'll have a lovely time," said Auntie Fan.

When his parents had driven away, Martin and Auntie Fan made some spaghetti sauce out of what she'd got and what Martin had brought from home. After they'd eaten, and Fergus had finished up the leftovers, they played Martin's favourite game, Ferret Flyover.

This involved
building a kind
of adventure
playground out
of tables and

chairs and
trays and
books and
cardboard

rolls and a
drainpipe, and
Fergus ran
through it all

like a fast car until he got tired
and wouldn't play any more.
Then he went to sleep in an
old slipper with his tail over
his nose, and Martin went to
bed as well.

Chapter Three

The next morning, Martin and
Auntie Fan and Fergus went
into town in her old van, which

the neighbours said was a
disgrace, to do some shopping.

Fergus caused a woman to scream in the supermarket when he ran down Auntie Fan's sleeve to see what she was getting from the meat counter, and Martin had to take him outside, because the manager was quite cross.

There was a bit of a scene in a cafe, too, when Fergus wanted to share a sausage roll being eaten by a man with a briefcase.

The man tried to hit him with his umbrella, but some-how knocked Auntie Fan's hat off instead. Two girls at the next table thought he was try-ing to mug her, so they leapt up, grabbed his umbrella,

tied him up with a tablecloth, then sat on him. People rushed out shouting for the police, and the police rushed in and a lot of coffee got spilt, and the owner of the cafe was tearing his hair and it took quite some time to get everything settled again.

Somehow Martin and Auntie Fan and Fergus found themselves outside in the street. "What a funny place," said Auntie Fan. "At the cafe by the bus station they all like Fergus. Aren't people odd?" And Martin agreed that they were.

That evening,
Mr Small
came round.
He lived in
the nearest of
the houses with
the big lawns, and he
was looking serious. "I think
I ought to warn you," he said,
"that a lot of us round here
have been

burgled."
Auntie Fan
looked
sympathetic
and said,
"What a
shame."

26

Mr Small glanced round the room, where several of the chairs were upside down because Martin had been playing Ferret Flyover again, and pursed his lips. "We are all very concerned about security," he said. "Do you, for instance, have bolts on your windows and a burglar alarm?"

"No," said Auntie Fan. "But then I don't have anything worth stealing. Only the TV – and that blew up last week."

Mr Small shook his head. "That's not the point," he said. "Burglars don't know what there is to steal until they're inside your house, do they? And a house like this, with no security whatsoever, simply encourages them. There are certain standards to be kept up." His face got quite pink. "And I really must say," he went on, "some of us feel that your house – how shall I put this – lowers the tone of the district."

Auntie Fan blinked in surprise, but said nothing.

"That dreadful van," said Mr Small. "And the weeds.

And – the ferret. Ferrets are not nice. They smell."

"So do people," said Auntie Fan. "Horrible aftershave – it makes my eyes run."

Mr Small, who smelt quite strongly of aftershave himself, turned pinker than ever, and Martin thought he'd better change the subject. 'Do *you* have a pet?" he asked.

"I have
tropical fish,"
said Mr Small.
"They're
very nice."

"But you can't take them out
for rides or wear them round
your neck," Auntie Fan pointed
out. "They're no *fun* are they?"

"I don't like fun," said Mr
Small. "And that ferret of yours
bit Mrs Ponsonby. She was only
collecting for the fête."

"She sat on him," said
Auntie Fan. "There he was,
curled up on a chair, minding
his own business, and this
huge woman sat on him.

Anyway, it was only a tiny nip – I'm surprised she noticed."

Mr Small glared at Fergus, who had appeared over the back of the sofa at that moment, and said, "Well, it had better not happen again."

"Oh it won't," said Auntie Fan. "Next time, Mrs Ponsonby can stay on the doorstep."

When Mr Small had gone, Martin said, "I think you and Fergus ought to move somewhere nicer. Where people are friendly."

"Somewhere less Nice you mean," agreed Auntie Fan. "Yes, you may be right."

Then Martin had a brainwave. "Hey – the flat under ours is empty! Mrs Handy moved away. It would be great if you were just downstairs – I'd see Fergus every day, not just when there's an emergency."

"That could be quite a good idea," said Auntie Fan.

"I'll give it some serious thought." Then, as it was getting quite late, they went off to bed, leaving Fergus curled up in his old slipper in front of the kitchen stove.

Chapter Four

In the middle
of the night,
Martin woke
suddenly.

He was sure he'd heard a
noise – some sort of creak or
shuffle. He lay in the darkness,
listening so hard that his ears
whistled.

Then he heard it again, a stealthy, heavy sound of something being moved. After a pause, it came again, with a slight clunk and rattle before it stopped. Someone had opened a drawer in the kitchen table where the knives and forks were kept, then closed it again, trying not to make a noise. A burglar.

Martin got quietly out of bed and crept to the door, silently pulled it open, and tiptoed to Auntie Fan's room. He slipped through her door and went over to her bed. "Auntie Fan!" he breathed.

"Auntie Fan! Wake up – I think we're being burgled."

"Mmmm?" said Auntie Fan. "What time is it?"

She reached for the bedside light, but Martin stopped her. "It's a *burglar*," he whispered. "Downstairs. Opening drawers. What shall we do?"

"Oh dear, I don't know," said Auntie Fan, waking up properly. "Do you suppose he's dangerous?" She got out of bed and put on her dressing gown. She and Martin crept to the top of the stairs – and at that moment there was a blood-curdling scream from the kitchen.

Auntie Fan switched on the light and rushed down the stairs with Martin at her heels and flung open the kitchen door. There, in the middle of the floor, a young man with a lot of tattoos and earrings was doing a wild dance, shaking his legs and clutching his trousers and still uttering shrieks.

"Aha," said Auntie Fan. "This looks to me like a case of Ferret Up The Trousers." She marched across to the burglar and said, "Stop jumping about, silly boy. Stand still."

The burglar did as he was told, though he was so scared that all his tattoos twitched.

"Martin, dear, look in the fridge and see if you can find something tasty," Auntie Fan said. "We need something to tempt him with. Fergus, I mean."

"There's a sardine," said Martin, "but it looks a bit old."

"Perfect," said Auntie Fan. "He'll love that." She bent down and held the sardine in front of the burglar's very dirty trainer.

"Come along, Fergus," she cooed. "Nice sardine – come and see."

The burglar shut his eyes, and trembled even more.

After a pause, Fergus emerged whiskers first, from the bottom of his jeans, and gobbled up the sardine, after which Martin picked him up and stroked him.

"Flippin' 'Enry," said the burglar. "A flamin' ferret. Now, that's not playin' fair. I mean, what next? Crocodiles?"

There was a banging at the front door and when Martin went to open it with Fergus on his shoulder, there stood Mr Small.

"I was – er – watching a video," he said. "The wife had gone to bed. And I heard screams. Is anything the matter?"

"No, we're fine," said Martin. "Fergus caught a burglar, that's all. Come in."

He led Mr Small back to the kitchen, where the burglar was still going on about ferrets. "I mean, locks and bolts and systems is OK, you expect them, everyone's got systems. Dogs is dodgy but you can carry a cold sausage and hope for the best, but ferrets – secret weapon, innit." He turned to Mr Small. " 'Ave you got one of them an' all?"

"Oh, yes," said Mr Small promptly. "Every house in the road has its ferret. We wouldn't be without them."

The burglar shook his head. "I give up," he said. "That's the end, that is. You and your ferrets, you've put me out of business. No more crime – I'm going straight, so help me. Down the Job Centre in the morning." And he climbed out of the window, which he had left open when he came in, and disappeared into the night.

"That was not true," Martin said sternly to Mr Small. "You haven't got a ferret."

Mr Small blushed slightly. "No," he admitted. "But I *could* have had one. Couldn't I?" He turned to Auntie Fan. "I wonder, dear lady, if you could put me in touch with a supplier of these creatures?"

"I don't think so," said Auntie Fan. "I'm going to move away, you see. I'm sure you'll understand why."

Mr Small turned even pinker and said, "Oh, don't do that. I was a little hasty in what I said. I take it all back.

Come to our coffee morning –
Thursday, eleven-thirty. I'm
sure my wife will be delighted.
And bring – ah – Fergus."

"Too late," said Auntie Fan.
"But you could put up a
notice saying,

It might work for a bit."

"But not for long, if we
don't have any ferrets," said
Mr Small.

"I'd much rather you were staying." He reached out his finger to pat Fergus on the head,

then thought better of it and went home to watch the rest of his video.

Chapter Five

Martin, Fergus and Auntie Fan
slept late the next morning
after their disturbed
night,   and had a
long and
leisurely
breakfast.
Then they
talked
about the
move to the
flat below Martin's,
and drew plans of it,
working out where Auntie
Fan's furniture would fit.

They took Fergus for a walk,
then had tea, and Martin's
mother phoned to say they
were back, so he could go
home. Auntie Fan took him in
the van, together with Fergus.

When they arrived, they
found that the lift wasn't
working, so the three of them
climbed up the eighteen
flights of stairs to Martin's flat.

By the time they got there,
Auntie Fan was scarlet in the
face and gasping for breath,
and couldn't say a word.

Martin's parents weren't much better. They had spent the whole weekend lying in a ditch with a hundred and forty other people who wanted to see the flat-footed mudwit, but it had gone somewhere else. They looked damp and dirty.

"We had a burglar!" said Martin, "but Fergus caught him. And hey, Auntie Fan's coming to live downstairs! So Fergus can visit us every day.

Isn't it great?"

Nobody said anything.
Auntie Fan was still speechless
after the stairs and Martin's
parents seemed a bit subdued.
"I'll put the kettle on," said
Martin. And when he'd done
that, he went to see the budgies, with Fergus draped round
his shoulders.

Beeb and Ighty were
sitting side by side on
their perch as usual,
watching a game show,
but at the sight of
Fergus they shrieked
and chattered and flew
madly round the room,

knocking things
off the mantel-
piece and
squawking like fire
alarms. Martin's
mother ran in to
see what the fuss
was about and
said, "*Martin* ! Take that
horrible animal out of here!"

"Sorry," said Martin. His mum had grass in her hair, but he decided not to mention it right then. He carried Fergus into his bedroom, and fished in his pocket for the big fly he'd caught in Auntie Fan's van. Mrs Toffee came rushing out at the sight of it, but Fergus was quicker. He grabbed the fly and ate it, and the way he looked at Mrs Toffee, Martin could see he wouldn't mind eating her as well. And that could be a problem with Fergus as a daily visitor. Maybe ferrets didn't mix with budgies and spiders.

Thoughtfully, Martin took Fergus back to the kitchen, where Auntie Fan had recovered a bit. "That lift," she was gasping. "Does it *ever* work?"

"Not often," said Martin's mum. "We don't mind, it keeps us fit for the bird-watching."

"I don't think I want to be fit," said Auntie Fan. "Not that fit, anyway."

Martin looked at her. "You mean you're not going to come," he said.

"It's not just the stairs,"
Auntie Fan said. "I'm really
sorry, dear, but – I'd miss
the weeds, you know. The
balcony's all right for a few
plants in pots, but there's no
room for weeds, is there?"

"No, suppose not," said
Martin. He went and stared
out of the window, trying
hard not to feel disappointed.

It would have been so nice to have Fergus just downstairs, even if he didn't come up for visits.

Martin's dad came over to make the tea. "Don't look so miserable," he said.

Martin shrugged. A bird whizzed past the window, but he took no notice.

"You're not really into bird-watching, are you?" said his dad.

"Not really," said Martin.

"Funny that – can't see why you don't enjoy it," his dad remarked, brushing at some mud on his sleeve.

"I think perhaps I'm more of an animal-watcher" said Martin.

His dad nodded slowly. "That makes sense," he said, "Yes, I can understand that. Well, look – what if we get you a dog? Just a very small one that can't look out of the window and scare the birds?"

"Hey,"breathed Martin. "Really?" A small dog wouldn't scare Mrs Toffee, either."

"Yes, really," his dad said, nodding. "Fred Pipit was next to me in the ditch this weekend and he was saying his small dog's just had puppies. Fred's trying to find homes for them. His budgies like his dog, he says. They talk to it."

"Well, that's something," said Martin's mother as she got the milk out of the fridge. "Maybe ours would start talking if we had a dog."

"They'd probably bark," said Auntie Fan. Martin's mother looked pleased. "That would be good," she said.

"A dog and
two budgies
all barking –
a terrific
burglar
alarm.

I hadn't bothered about it
before, but after your nasty
experience this weekend –"

Martin glanced at Auntie Fan, who was smiling to herself as if she'd thought of something funny. "What about Mr Small and his burglar-proofing?" he asked. "Are you going to find him a ferret?"

"I was just thinking," said Auntie Fan. "I might get a little wife for Fergus and they can have some ferret babies. Then I can supply everyone in the road. Yes, that's what I'll do – set up as a ferret breeder."

"Mr Small will like that,"
said Martin.

"Yes, won't he?" agreed
Auntie Fan. And her smile
grew broader as she took a
biscuit from the
tin and broke a bit
off for Fergus,
who ran down
Martin's sleeve to
get it.

Martin smiled
as well. Even if
Auntie Fan wasn't downstairs,
there'd always be emergencies
when he could go and stay
with her and the ferret family –
and take his dog.

Maybe he'd call it Burglar and teach the budgies to say its name. Then they'd shout it all the time. His mum would like that – yes, she'd be really pleased. Altogether, Martin thought, things had worked out beautifully, thanks to Auntie Fan. And of course to Fergus, the fabulous, burglar-catching ferret!